Oh, My Lucky Stars!

May all your
wishes come true!
Valerie Hanks - Goetz

Oh, My Lucky Stars!

by

Valerie Hanks Goetz

Riverhaven Books
www.RiverhavenBooks.com

Oh, My Lucky Stars is not a work of fiction; any similarity regarding names, characters, or incidents is entirely intentional. This story is based on real happenings and serves as evidence that wishes can come true.

Published in the United States by Riverhaven Books
www.RiverhavenBooks.com

ISBN: 978-1-937588-30-4

Printed in the United States of America
by Country Press,
Lakeville, Massachusetts

This book

is dedicated

to all those people

who take in strays.

With special thanks

to my husband, Tom, for all his support and insight,

to my children, Cassie, Allen, and Jeromey, for all their skills they put at my disposal,

to Staci Caver for challenging me to write this book,

to Rev. Judith Campbell for her mentoring,

and to Stephanie Blackman, for her guidance and patience as my publisher,

and, finally, to my grandchildren, Alexis, Samantha, Elliott, Annabelle, and Benjamin, for being my everyday inspiration.

And this is the way it was told to me......

once there were two sisters,
Alexis who was ten and Samantha who was eight.

They lived in Seattle, Washington, and every summer they would fly to Arkansas to visit their grandparents, Dadoo and Bo-Chee.

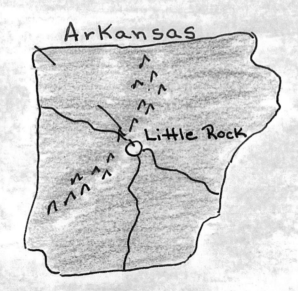

Dadoo and Bo-Chee had a big backyard with a pond,
lots of trees, two dogs, and four cats.

When they would visit, Samantha and Alexis would take horseback riding lessons, swim, kayak, hike, and create art in Bo-chee's studio.

Alexis loved horses!
Samantha loved having so much space at Dadoo and Bo-chee's to play with all of the animals!

After returning home from spending the summer with Dadoo and Bo-Chee, one evening at bedtime Alexis asked her father, "Can I have a horse?"

As he tucked the bed covers around her, he answered, "I am sorry, Alexis; our yard is too small for a horse."

Samantha asked her father, "Can we have a bigger backyard?"

Her father sadly replied, "I am sorry, Samantha, but we can't make our yard any bigger."

As he kissed each girl on the cheek goodnight, he said, "But if you see a star fall from the sky, make a wish on it and maybe the wish will come true." He left the window open so the girls could see the night sky.

Just after he closed the door, a star

F
E
L
L!

"OH, MY LUCKY STARS!"
both girls exclaimed and quickly made a wish.

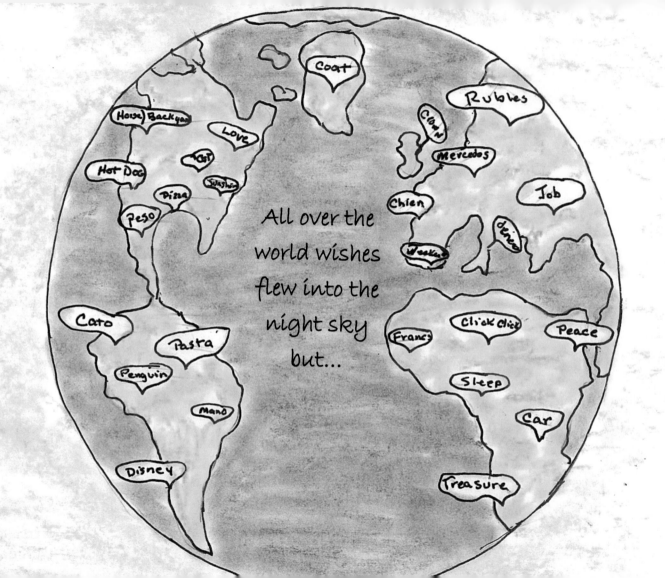

The Wish Fairy bonked her head on the star when it fell.

As she reached down to pick a wish, she accidentally grabbed two wishes and smashed them together. The wish she granted was...

part Alexis's wish and part Samantha's wish.

Bark?
Bark?

Woof!
Woof!

"What was that noise?"
barked the dogs.
"Who made that sound?"
meowed the cats.

Meow?
Meow?

Purrr.
Purrr.

"Did you hear that?" asked Dadoo.

"Did the sound come from our backyard?" replied Bo-Chee.

And they all ran to the backyard where they found...

"Alexisamantha's lucky wish," he read.
"Who is Alexisamantha?"

"Could this be our Alexis and Samantha's
names together?" puzzled Bo-Chee. "Let's give
the girls a call in the morning."

"Hi, Alexis and Samantha! We have a big surprise in our backyard...it's a horse with a tag labeled, 'Alexisamantha's lucky wish'," said Dadoo and Bo-Chee.

Alexis
and
Samantha
... Calling ...

"Oh, my lucky stars!" shrieked the girls in unison.
"I saw a falling star last night!" yelled Alexis.
"Me too!" shouted Samantha.
"I wished for a horse," added Alexis.
"I wished for a big backyard like Dadoo and Bo-Chee," exclaimed Samantha.

Dadoo congratulated, "Both of your wishes came true!!!"
"Hmmmm......this is one lucky horse!" Bo-chee proclaimed.
"We should name him Lucky!"

And they did!

The end.

Watch for more tales about Lucky,

his family, and

The Truth About February

coming soon to stores and electronic devices near you

because wishes do come true!